Famous Fairy Tales

Famous Fairy Tales

Adapted by Fred Ladd
and Murray Benson

GROSSET & DUNLAP
A FILMWAYS COMPANY
Publishers • New York

Library of Congress Catalog Card No. 78-53666

ISBN: 0-448-14728-9 (Trade Edition)
ISBN: 0-448-13485-3 (Library Edition)

Contents

The Wild Swans

(Hans Christian Andersen, Denmark)

In a faraway land, where swallows fly for the winter, lived a king who had eleven sons and one daughter, Elise. The eleven brothers—they were all princes—and their sister were very happy together; but their happiness was soon to come to an end.

Their father, the king, married a woman who was beautiful, but wicked. She was, in fact, a sorceress who was not at all kind to the children. It did not take her long to make the king believe so many evil things about the boys that he began to care little for them.

One day, as the boys were playing, the wicked queen said, "Fly out into the world and look after yourselves! You shall fly about like birds without voices!"

But she could not cause things to be as bad for them as she would have liked—they turned into eleven beautiful wild swans! They flew out of the palace window, right across the park, the woods, and the sea!

The queen would willingly have turned Elise into a wild swan, too, but dared not do it at once, for the king wanted to see his daughter.

Poor Elise wept, and went out to look for her brothers. She wandered about all day, crossing meadows and marshes, till at last the beautiful open sea lay before her. How was she ever to go any farther?

Eleven white swans' feathers were lying on the sand, still with drops of water on them. Elise

picked them up, then looked at the sea. "With all its rolling, the sea is untiring," she thought. "I will be just as untiring! Thank you for your lesson, you rolling waves! Some time, my heart tells me, you will bear me to my beloved brothers!"

It was very lonely there by the shore, but Elise did not feel it, for the sea was ever-changing. She ate wild berries and found trees whose branches were bending with the weight of their own fruit. She went to a sparkling spring and drank water out of the hollow of her hand. In this way, one day passed like another.

Soon Elise was fifteen and a more beautiful royal child than she could not be found in all the world!

One day, when the sun was just about to go down, Elise saw eleven wild swans with golden crowns upon their heads flying toward the shore. She hid behind a bush as the swans settled close by. Then, as soon as the sun had sunk beneath the water, the swans shed their feathers and became eleven handsome princes—Elise's brothers! She sprang into their arms and called each by name!

How happy the princes were when they recognized their sister, and saw that she had grown so big and beautiful! They laughed and cried and talked for hours!

"We brothers," said the eldest, "have to fly about as swans as long as the sun is above the horizon. When it goes down, we regain our human shapes. So we always have to look for a resting place near sunset, for if we should happen to be flying among the clouds when the sun goes down, we would be hurled to the depths below!

"We are forced to live in a land beyond the sea—a beautiful land, but not our own dear home. Our flight takes two of the longest days in the year, yet there is not a single island on the way where we can spend the night; there is only a little rock that juts above the water midway through our journey. There we spend the night in our human form!

"We are permitted to come back

here only once a year to see the palace where we were born, and the place where our mother is buried. Then we must fly away again across the ocean."

"How can I free you?" asked Elise.

"If only we could take you with us!" said her eldest brother. "Tomorrow we must fly away, not to return for another year. But we can't leave you like this! Have you the courage to go with us?"

"Oh, yes! Yes!" cried Elise. "Take me with you!"

The brothers then wove a net of elastic willow bark and strong rushes. Elise lay down upon it. When the sun rose and the brothers became swans again, they gathered the net in their bills and flew high above the open sea! All day long they flew, but they went slower than usual, for now they had their sister to carry.

Evening was approaching. Elise saw the sun beginning to sink and she felt terror in her heart, for the solitary rock was nowhere in sight! The swans seemed to be taking stronger strokes, desperate to reach the rock before sunset when they would become human again.

Black clouds gathered and strong winds announced the coming of a storm. The sun was now at the edge of the sea. Elise's heart trembled, for still no rock was to be seen and the poor girl feared they would all be hurled into the sea!

Then suddenly the swans plunged downward! Half the sun was below the horizon. There, for the first time, Elise saw the little rock below, a rock that looked no bigger than the head of a dolphin above water. Her feet touched solid earth just as the sun disappeared and the brothers regained their human form!

There was barely enough room for them all. Storm-tossed waves beat upon the rock and washed over them like drenching rain. Lightning flashed and thunder roared. Elise and her brothers held each other's hands and sang psalms to give them comfort and courage through the night.

When dawn came, the air was

pure and still. As soon as the sun rose, the swans flew off with Elise. Once again, they flew all day until at last Elise could see a beautiful land before her. Blue mountains with cedar woods and palaces rose high into the air. Before the sun set, Elise was sitting among the hills in front of a large cave covered with delicate green vines. There she was to sleep.

That night, praying that she might dream of a way to free her brothers, she fell asleep and soon a dazzling fairy appeared.

"Your brothers can be made free," the fairy said, "but have you courage and endurance enough for it? You must pluck the stinging nettles that grow only near the cave where you sleep, and in church-yards. Mark that! Those you may pluck, though they will burn and blister your hands! Crush the nettles and you will have flax; of this you must weave eleven coats of mail. Throw these over the wild swans and the spell will be broken. But from the moment you begin work until you finish—even if it takes years—you must not utter a sound, or your brothers will die!"

The fairy seemed to touch Elise's hand. It felt like burning fire, and woke Elise. Seeing bright daylight, she left the cave to begin her work at once. She found the prickly nettles and seized them. How they hurt her fingers! Great blisters rose on her hands and arms. But she uttered not a single sound; she suffered willingly if only it would free her beloved brothers. She crushed every nettle with her bare feet, and twisted it into green flax.

When her brothers returned that night, they were alarmed to find their sister mute; they thought it must be another spell cast by their wicked stepmother. But when they saw Elise's hands, they understood she was doing it for their sakes and they wept.

On the following day, Elise finished the first coat of mail and was just beginning the next when suddenly a hunting horn sounded among the mountains. Big dogs appeared at the opening to the cave and barked loudly. In a few minutes, the hunting party arrived, led by the handsome young king of the country! Never had he seen so lovely a girl.

"How did you come here?" he asked. Elise covered her hands to hide the wounds and bowed her head, but dared not speak.

"You cannot stay here," said the king. "Come with me. If you're as good as you are beautiful, I'll put a golden crown on your head. You shall live in my palace!" He lifted her upon his horse and rode back to the palace. Elise wept and wrung her hands. If only she might speak!

The palace was splendid, but Elise had no eyes for it. She only sorrowed as women dressed her in royal robes, placed pearls in her hair, and drew gloves over her blistered hands. Finally, the king appeared and led her to a little chamber close by the room where she was to sleep. It was adorned with green carpets and made to resemble the cave where he found her. On the floor lay the bundle of flax she had spun from nettles, and from the ceiling hung the coat of mail she had finished.

When Elise saw these things, she smiled for the first time. Blood rushed back to her cheeks. She thought of the freedom of her brothers and kissed the king's hand. The king in turn lifted her, pressed her to his heart, and ordered church bells to peal to announce his forthcoming marriage to the lovely mute girl from the woods! They were married soon after; Elise became the beautiful queen of the country.

In her eyes was love for the good and handsome king who did all he could to please her. Each day she grew more and more devoted to him, and longed to confide in him, but she knew that to do so would mean the death of her brothers. Each night she stole into the chamber the king had decorated for her and wove one coat after another. Then, when she came to the seventh, all her flax was used up; she knew she would have to pick more nettles from a churchyard.

That night, Elise's wicked stepmother arrived at the palace. The sorceress, who had turned the eleven brothers into wild swans and forced them to live in the young king's country, knew that the spell would soon be broken by Elise. And so now she had come with a plan to save the spell and do away with Elise at the same time. She spoke in private with the king.

"Don't be deceived by the queen's beauty and her silence, Your Majesty," said the sorceress. "Elise is a witch! Even now, she sits in her chamber weaving coats of nettles. Who but a witch would do that?"

The king refused to listen. Then the sorceress told him that Elise gathered nettles in the churchyard at night, an evil practice the king could see with his own eyes. At that, two big tears rolled down the king's cheeks. Doubt had crept into his heart.

Elise was by now stealing down into the moonlit garden and through long alleys that led to a churchyard where the nettles grew. She felt as much terror as if she were doing some evil deed. The king and the sorceress followed her. They saw her hesitate at

the gates to the churchyard, then slip inside.

"You see, Your Majesty?" whispered the sorceress. "There she is, on her knees amongst the gravestones—like a ghoul!" The king turned his head away.

"The people must judge her," he said, and the people judged, "Let the witch be consumed in the flames!"

Elise was led to a dark, damp dungeon. She was scornfully given her bundle of nettles and her coats of mail to lay her head upon. They could have given her nothing more precious!

She set to work again with many prayers. She had only this night to finish her work, or else all would be wasted; in the morning, she would die, and her brothers remain wild swans forever.

All night long, she continued to weave the coats of mail. Her fingers never flew more quickly!

In the morning, the entire populace streamed to the town square to see the witch-burning. A miserable horse drew the cart in which Elise sat, unceasingly weaving the green yarn. Even on her way to her death, amid scoffing insults from the crowd, Elise could not abandon her unfinished work. Ten coats lay completed at her feet; she labored away at the eleventh.

In the center of the square, a huge woodpile had been built for the burning. Elise was led atop the pile, and still she kept on weaving. Flaming torches were brought, and still she wove!

Just then, eleven white swans suddenly appeared and flew down. Elise hastily threw eleven coats of mail into the air. The swans flew into them and were immediately transformed into eleven handsome princes!

"Now I may speak!" cried Elise. "I am innocent!" At that moment the sorceress, her magic destroyed, shriveled into nothingness.

"The queen is innocent! She is innocent!" shouted the crowd.

"Yes, she is innocent!" said the

eldest brother. He told the king and the people all that had happened.

While he spoke, a fragrance of flowers suddenly filled the air; the woodpile had taken root and sprouted hosts of red roses!

Church bells began to ring of their own accord. Singing birds flocked around them. Joy, at last, was in Elise's heart. Hand in hand with her husband, she returned to the palace. Such a procession no king had seen in any land!

The Ears of King Midas

(Greek Mythology)

High atop Mount Olympus lived two gods, Pan and Apollo, who were always quarreling. Pan, who played the pipes, thought he was a better musician than Apollo. Apollo, who strummed a lyre, thought he was a better musician than Pan.

When one god could no longer tolerate the playing of the other, he would begin playing so loudly upon his own instrument, to drown out the other, that the other gods on Mount Olympus would complain of the din!

At last, to settle the argument, Pan and Apollo decided to go down from the Mount and ask a man well known for his honesty. That man was the good King, Midas. They appeared before him one day and explained what they wanted Midas to do.

First, Apollo strummed his lyre.

Then Pan played his pipes.

Each played as skillfully as he could. When both had finished, and Midas was considering his choice, Apollo whispered in the King's ear, "Say that I am the better musician or I'll punish you."

Midas thought them both good, but he did prefer one to the other and was too honest to say otherwise. "I prefer the plain sounds of Pan's pipes," he said.

Pan thanked the King and returned happily to Mount Olympus. But Apollo was angry. He returned to the Mount and thought, "How shall I punish a man who is honest, but stubborn as a mule?" Suddenly, he knew the perfect punishment! He pointed a finger at Midas's castle and commanded, "Midas, have the ears of a mule! The ears of a mule!"

King Midas was in his chamber when, suddenly, he felt his ears growing! He ran to his mirror, then fell back in horror at what he saw there. "My ears!" he gasped. "They're the ears of a mule! This must be Apollo's work!"

The sight of those ears was loathsome. Midas tried to tuck them out of sight beneath his crown, but to no avail—they were too large. He began to think of what it would mean to face life with the ears of a mule. Would not his own subjects laugh at him?

Just then, the King's doctor, his jeweler, and his barber arrived for their appointment. They knocked upon the door of the chamber. "How can I face them?" thought Midas. He crawled into bed and pulled the cover over his head.

Hearing no reply, the doctor cautiously opened the door to the King's chamber and peered inside.

"Your Majesty?" he inquired. "We're here for our appointment. . . ."

"It's cancelled," replied the King. "Go away."

Instead, the faithful doctor approached the bed. "You're not feeling well, are you? As the royal physician, I should give you an examination." He reached out to remove the cover from the King's head, but quickly withdrew when Midas ordered, "Don't come near me!"

What strange behavior was this!

The jeweler, seeking to put the King in a better humor, stepped forward and said, "Your Majesty, I shall present you with a diamond the size of the egg of a pigeon!" But the King demanded, "What would I do with a diamond the size of the egg of a pigeon?"

For a moment there was stunned silence. Then the barber stepped forward and suggested, "Your Majesty, if I cut your hair very short, that might help to lift your spirits." Lift his spirits, indeed! Rather, his secret would surely come out! "No haircut!" shouted the King. "Now, all of you, get out! Leave me!"

The doctor, the jeweler, and the barber left. When he was alone again, Midas got out of his bed and walked once more to the mirror. He saw that the mule's ears were still there. He despaired. How could he hide them? Suddenly, he remembered a battle helmet he once had worn. The helmet was a high one and came to a point. Surely that would cover his ears.

He found the helmet and put it on. Indeed, it hid his ears so completely, the King was certain that no one would ever guess his secret!

But as he walked through a corridor, Midas overheard his faithful minister whispering to the jeweler, "You say he shouted at you? Impossible! Midas is known as the gentle king."

"Something must have happened to him!" whispered the jeweler.

"Is it possible," wondered Midas, "that the jeweler knows

about the mule's ears? I had better put him in prison to be certain he whispers no more about me!" And, indeed, Midas promptly ordered the jeweler put into a cell.

After that, the King never removed his helmet. He wore it all day; he wore it while he ate; he even slept in it!

He imprisoned everyone who even mentioned his name, till at last every cell was full! He trusted no one, not even his faithful doctor!

"Your Majesty," pleaded the doctor one day, "surely you have some strange illness. Allow me to examine you."

"Do you dare to speak so insolently to me, doctor?" demanded the King. "Guards, throw the doctor into the dungeon!" The poor doctor was thrown into a dark, damp cell beneath the castle.

Months passed, during which the King's hair grew longer and longer. Foreign diplomats came and were shocked; they hurried home, surprised by the shaggy appearance of the King! But Midas

cared little about official matters any more. His only concern was that people might laugh at him.

Then one day he thought, "I'm afraid the time has come. If my hair grows any longer, the people will surely grow suspicious. I must have my hair cut."

The barber was summoned. Then all the servants were sent away, leaving the King and the barber alone. The barber, who loved to gossip, cheerfully removed the King's helmet and began to chatter. But no sooner had he lifted a lock of the King's hair than he uncovered two long, furry ears!

The barber gasped! He knew he had seen what he ought not to have seen! The King knew it, too. "Barber," he said, "if you so much as speak one syllable of this to anyone, I shall have you beheaded! Understand?"

The barber was trembling with fear. "Y-y-your Majesty," he stammered, "I promise never to tell anyone that you have the ears of a jackass!"

"The ears of a mule," the King corrected him. "Now finish your work, and remember what will happen if you break your promise!"

When the barber left the royal palace and returned to town, the townspeople thronged around him. They begged him to tell them how the King looked. The barber refused. "Tell us," someone in the crowd pleaded, "is it true the King has grown horns on his head?"

"I can't tell you!" shouted the barber, and he hurried back to his shop. But the townspeople were curious. Every day they came to the barber's shop and asked questions about the King. The barber was eager to gossip and share his secret with them, but he dared not. He kept remembering the King's warning.

Finally, however, he could bear it no more. He simply had to tell the secret somehow. One night, he crept to a spot near the river, dug a hole in the ground, and into the hole he whispered, "King Midas has the ears of a mule! King Midas has the ears of a mule!" Then he

quickly covered over the hole! He felt better at once. He was relieved and happy. Thinking he had buried the secret forever, the barber left.

But soon marsh grass grew on the spot. When wind seethed through the tall grass, the grass swayed back and forth. As it swayed, the grass whispered, "King Midas has the ears of a mule! King Midas has the ears of a mule!"

The secret passed to trees nearby. Their rustling leaves could be heard to say, "King Midas has the ears of a mule! King Midas has the ears of a mule!"

Treetops rocking to and fro almost seemed to shout it out! "KING MIDAS HAS THE EARS OF A MULE! KING MIDAS HAS THE EARS OF A MULE!"

One night, a strong wind blew the secret to the edge of the woods. From there it was borne through the streets of the town. Townspeople opened their windows and heard, "King Midas has the ears of a mule! King Midas has the ears of a mule!"

The secret spread to the palace itself! "King Midas has the ears of a mule! King Midas has the ears of a mule!" The startled King looked to see who was revealing his secret. Nothing was there but the wind!

"This is the barber's work!", the King said in a rage. "For blabbering the secret, he shall pay with his head!" He started to summon the barber, but then he stopped and thought, "No, I cannot punish him. In all honesty, I myself am to blame for this."

The next day, Midas summoned his entire kingdom to the palace. When his subjects arrived, they found the King waiting for them upon a balcony of the palace, wearing the pointed helmet. He raised his arm to call for silence. "My loyal subjects," he began, "I want to show you something I should have shown you long ago!"

He removed the helmet, and there, for all to see, were the ears of a mule! A thousand gasps arose from the crowd!

"Yes," continued the King, sadly, "the ears of a mule— punishment bestowed upon me by the god Apollo for speaking the truth! To hide my shame, I com-

mitted many terrible deeds and acted in a manner unworthy of your King."

Midas had decided to give up his throne; but suddenly he was interrupted by a deep, booming voice from above commanding, "Wait, Midas!"

"Who is it?" Midas demanded of the intruder. "Who speaks?"

From out of the clouds appeared the mighty god, Jupiter! "Apollo will be punished," he said, "for foolishly wreaking his revenge upon you!" He pointed to King Midas. "And you were wrong to punish those who might have guessed your secret. But you spared the barber's life when he revealed your secret, proving that you have learned the lesson of mercy; therefore, as you have spared, so you shall be spared!"

Jupiter raised his arm for a moment and, in that moment, Midas's ears returned to normal. "Thank you, Jupiter," Midas started to say, but the mighty figure had already vanished.

The King's faithful minister,

standing behind him on the balcony, said, "This proves that you have remained fair, just, and honorable at heart, Your Majesty. Please release all those who are still in prison and remain our good and gentle ruler."

The crowd shouted its approval. The grateful King did as he was bid, and agreed to remain on the throne. He vowed anew always to speak the truth. And till the end of his days, that is what he did.

The Contest Between the North Wind and the Sun

(Greek and African legend)

One fine day, long, long ago, the angry North Wind looked across the sky at his old rival, the smiling Sun.

The North Wind scowled. He scowled and he scowled. He scowled for a long time. Then finally, he said, "I am the strongest force in the world! People call you Mister Sunshine and seem to prefer you to me, but all you ever do is stay there and smile. What secret power do you have?"

"I don't know," replied the Sun, and it kept on smiling . . . making the North Wind all the more angry.

"Do you know how strong I am?" demanded the North Wind. "Just a tiny blast from me strikes fear in the heart of the animal kingdom! Large or small, they hide in their burrows—from the littlest squirrel to the mightiest bear!

"Even the silver wolf cringes in fear of my power! For I am the North Wind!

"With ease, I can blow upon Man's largest cities—and freeze them in a flash!

"I can blow up a storm that will whip the sea into waves huge enough to capsize even the sturdiest of ships . . . and send them to the bottom!

"Why, I can freeze the entire Earth, as I did during the Ice Age long ago!" The North Wind laughed mightily. "I am the North Wind," he roared, "surely the strongest force in the world!"

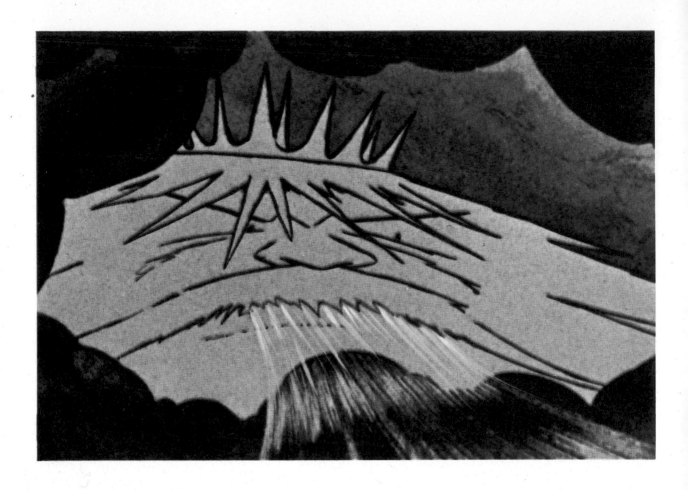

The Sun, still smiling, listened patiently to the North Wind boasting, then said, "Yes, you are strong . . . and it is true that many animals and some people do fear you. But that doesn't prove you're the strongest force in the world."

The North Wind scowled more than before. "Oh, it doesn't, eh? Who then is the strongest? You?"

"Well, I hate to brag," smiled the Sun, "but—"

The North Wind interrupted. "Ha!" he snorted. "Don't make me laugh! But we can settle this matter easily. Why not have a contest to find out which of us is stronger?"

At first, the Sun refused. But when the North Wind kept daring him, the Sun finally nodded and agreed, saying, "Very well. Let the contest begin."

Just then, a traveler and his mule appeared on a road below.

"Ah! What good luck!" said the North Wind. "Whichever one of us can cause that traveler to take off his coat is the stronger—agreed?"

"All right," sighed the Sun. "Agreed. You start first."

"Good!" chuckled the North

Wind, certain that he would win. "This won't take long."

The North Wind swooped down toward the traveler, took a deep breath, and then started to blow. Feeling a sudden chill, the traveler stopped and grasped the front of his coat.

"Ha!" laughed the North Wind. "That was easier than I expected. He's taking off his coat already." But the traveler did not remove his coat. Instead, he buttoned it.

The North Wind scowled. He blew harder.

The traveler pulled the hood on his coat over his head and drew the coat tightly around him.

Seeing that, the North Wind blew even harder!

But the stronger the wind blew, the tighter the traveler drew his coat!

The North Wind was beginning to run out of breath.

"Stubborn man!" he thought. "Defy me, will he? Well, I'll give him one blast with everything I've got!"

The North Wind took a deep, deep breath, then blew his most powerful blast, sending dark

storm clouds scudding across the sky. Leaves were torn from the branches of trees. Animals scurried for their burrows. The traveler's mule was carried high into the air, landing in an empty tree stump! The traveler himself struggled to keep from being blown away. He crouched on the ground like a squash and wrapped himself in his coat from head to toe!

At last the North Wind was exhausted. He could blow no more. With great effort, he climbed back above the storm clouds.

The Sun seemed amused. "Giving up already?" he asked.

"Certainly not!" gasped the North Wind. "Just . . . taking a little rest, that's all."

"Well," smiled the Sun, "you certainly are strong, but you don't seem to be able to make that traveler remove his coat. Now it's my turn. While you're resting, suppose I go down a bit and see what I can do. Is that all right with you?"

"Don't be silly," snapped the North Wind, feeling very grouchy indeed. "If I, with all my power,

can't make him take off his coat, then how are you going to do it?"

"Watch!" said the Sun. So saying, he dipped lower in the sky and sent a sunbeam to part the storm clouds raised by the North Wind. Then, softly, gently, the smiling Sun began brightening and warming the earth.

Slowly, the traveler rose. He was puzzled. He had never seen such strange weather! He began to breathe deeply and bask in the unexpected sunshine.

But the North Wind chuckled. "You can't do it, either. He's up,

but he hasn't taken off his coat!"

"Well, give me time, my friend, give me time!"

So saying, the Sun shone even brighter!

It was beginning to feel like spring! Flowers burst into bloom! Birds began to sing. Animals came out of their burrows. Butterflies even emerged from their cocoons!

At last, it grew so sunny and warm that the traveler took off his coat!

The North Wind scowled more than ever. But he said nothing.

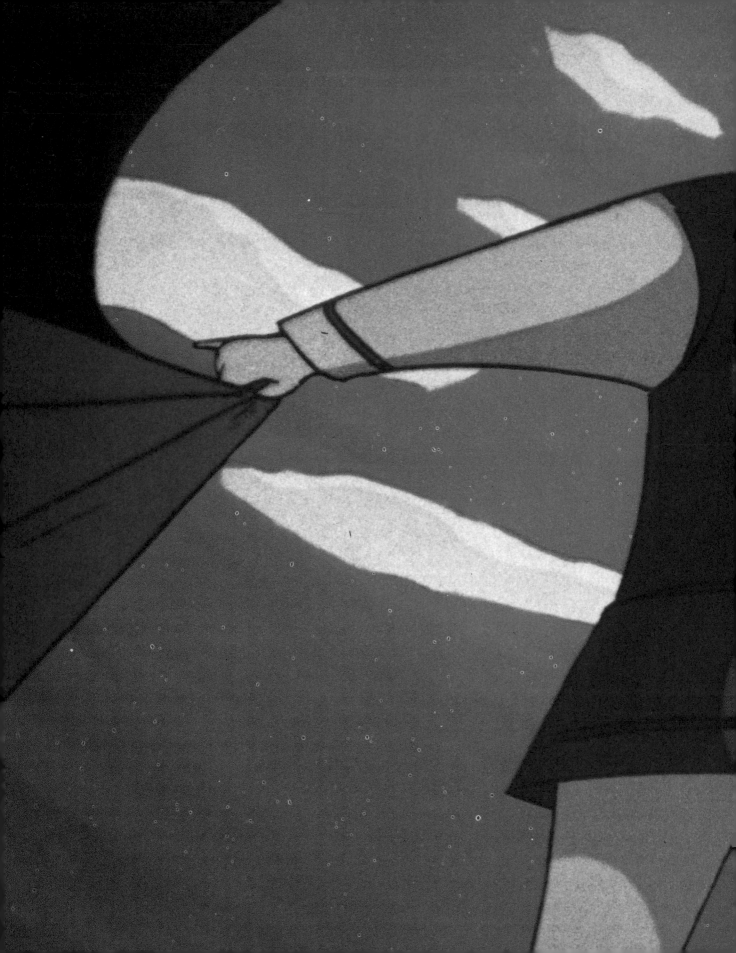

What was there to say? He had lost the contest.

The Sun had won.

Of course, that wasn't the end of the North Wind. Every year, to prove that he's still around and as strong as ever, he sends animals to the shelter of their burrows and freezes Man's largest cities. But the Sun, after watching patiently, comes along with a big smile, turning Winter into Spring and winning anew the ancient contest between North Wind and Sun.

The Little Match Girl

(Hans Christian Andersen, Denmark)

It was late on a bitterly cold New Year's Eve. The town was crowded with happy folk on their way home for a holiday dinner of roast goose. But there was a poor little girl who was not happy. She wandered alone in the cold, dark, snowy streets carrying a bundle of matches her father had given her to sell. "Matches . . . matches!" she called. Nobody had bought any from her all day long; nobody had given her so much as a penny.

She had been wearing slippers when she left home but they were not much good, for they were so huge. They had belonged to her mother. She ran across the street to avoid a swiftly moving carriage, and lost one slipper; it could not be found anywhere. So she had to go on with one foot bare. It soon turned blue with the cold.

In their bright, warm houses, people sang and celebrated the holiday. But in the cold, snowy streets, the little match girl called, "Matches . . . matches . . . please buy my matches. . . . " Shivering with cold and hunger, she tried to creep along, but her hands and feet were nearly frozen.

At last she came to a house where steps leading up to the front door offered some shelter from the icy wind. Here she crouched behind the steps, drawing her feet under her. Still, she felt colder than ever. She dared not go home, since she had sold no matches nor earned a single penny, and so her father would surely beat her. Be-

sides, it was almost as cold at home as it was here.

"My hands are nearly dead from the cold," she thought. "Oh, how much just one little match would warm them! If only I could take one from the bundle and light it. Father would be so angry, but—just one match. . . ."

She pulled one out and struck it against the steps. "Rish!" it sputtered. It burned like a little candle as the girl held her hand around it. Gazing into the flame, she imagined that she was sitting in front of a great iron stove . . . glowing hot! . . . a stove with shining brass feet and a golden cover! Then, just as the girl was stretching out her feet to warm them, the flame died out, the stove vanished, and she was left holding the end of a burnt-out match.

She removed another match from the bundle and struck it. "Rish!" Looking into the flame this time, the girl could see a room such as she had never seen before! On a table spread with a snowy cloth, fine china and crystal gob-

lets was a banquet elegant enough for a queen—steaming roast goose stuffed with apples and plums! Fresh ripe fruit and cherry tarts! As the little girl watched with delight, the goose leaped from its dish and danced right up to her—then the match flickered out and the banquet disappeared.

"Rish!" She struck another match. This time a tree seemed to grow from the flame, a Christmas tree glittering with thousands of lighted candles and decorated with dolls in colorful costumes! The lit-tle girl reached out for them—then out went the match. The tree slowly vanished, but the Christmas candles rose higher and higher till they reached the sky and became twinkling stars. Suddenly one of them fell, making a bright streak of light across the sky.

"A falling star!" thought the girl. "Someone is dying." The girl's old grandmother, now dead, the only person who had ever been kind to her, used to tell her that when a star fell, a soul was going to heaven.

The girl struck another match.

This time it was her grandmother who appeared in the flame, looking gentle and happy.

"Grandmother! Grandmother!" cried the little girl. "Oh, take me with you! I know you'll disappear when the match goes out. You'll vanish like the warm stove, the roast goose, and the Christmas tree!" She struck the whole bundle of matches, for she wished to keep her grandmother with her.

"I am with you now, my dear," her grandmother said. "Come." She had never looked more lovely. She lifted the little girl in her arms and they soared upward in a halo of light and joy! Up, up they flew, far above the earth, to where there was neither cold, nor hunger, nor pain—heaven!

In the cold morning light a crowd gathered at the spot where the little match girl had spent her last night on earth. She was sitting under the steps, frozen.

"Poor dear," someone said. "Look at all the burnt-out matches in her hand. She was trying to warm herself." She was smiling.

No one could imagine what beautiful things she had seen, nor how happily she had gone in a halo with her kind, lovely grandmother.

The Emperor's New Clothes

(Hans Christian Andersen, Denmark)

Many years ago, on the side of a hill, there stood a great city. Atop the hill, in a splendid castle, lived the Emperor. Now, this Emperor was exceedingly fond of new clothes. He spent all his money on being well-dressed. He cared nothing about reviewing his soldiers, or going for a ride in his carriage, except to show off his new clothes. Here it was rarely said, "The King is in the throne room," for he usually wasn't. And instead of saying, "The King is in council," as one might about any other ruler, here they always said, "The Emperor is in his dressing room." Most often, the vain Emperor could be found posing before his mirror in one new costume after another! He had a suit of clothes for every hour of the day!

Each day, many strangers came to the great city. Among them one day came two swindlers claiming to be magic weavers! They called upon the Emperor, and said they were able to weave the most beautiful cloth in the world. Not only were the colors and patterns breathtaking, they claimed, but the cloth itself was magic—it was invisible to those who were either unfit for their jobs or unusually stupid.

"Exactly the cloth for me!" thought the Emperor. "If I wore it, I'd be able to discover who in my kingdom is unfit for his post. I could also tell the wise from the foolish. I'll pay the weavers to start weaving new clothes for me at once!"

The swindlers set up a loom in a

little shop not far from the palace and pretended to weave. They didn't really weave because there was nothing on the loom. They burned candles far into the night as they worked on an empty loom, weaving nothing at all.

The next morning the Emperor thought, "I wonder what progress those weavers have made." He felt somewhat uneasy about going himself to check up on the weavers, remembering what they had said about the magic thread, so he ordered a faithful minister to go.

The minister was a sensible man who did his duty well.

When the minister arrived at the swindler's shop, he stared at the empty loom.

"Minister," said the swindlers, "please examine the texture of the cloth, the patterns, the pretty colors—aren't they priceless?"

The minister saw nothing, he felt nothing, he stared as hard as he dared at the empty loom. "Heaven help me!" he thought. "I can't see anything at all!" But he didn't dare say so. To admit to the swindlers

that he saw nothing would be to admit that he was unfit for his office, or stupid.

He imagined what the Emperor would say. The Emperor would surely discharge him! The minister would become the laughingstock of the kingdom! That would never do.

"Er . . . why, it's magnificent!" proclaimed the minister. "I'll report to the Emperor. He'll be delighted! This is a work of art!"

And that is what the minister reported to the Emperor.

Presently, the Emperor—still uneasy when he remembered that those unfit for office would not be able to see the fabric—decided to send another trustworthy minister to see how the work was progressing and when it would be ready.

The same thing happened to him that happened to the first minister.

He couldn't see anything on the loom, because there was nothing to see.

"Isn't it beautiful cloth?" asked the first swindler, pretending to drape some over his hands. As he did so, the second swindler explained all about the colors and patterns which, of course, were nowhere to be seen.

"I must not let them know I cannot see the cloth," thought the second minister. So he beamed happily and cried, "Why, this is exquisite! What beautiful colors! What lovely patterns! I'll tell the Emperor—at once!"

And that is exactly what the second minister did.

Soon, everyone in town began to talk about the splendid cloth the weavers were making for the Emperor's new clothes.

Now the Emperor could control his curiosity no longer. "I shall go to the weavers and inspect the fabric myself," he said.

Accompanied by the two ministers who had gone before, the Emperor went to the little shop where the swindlers were working as hard as ever on the imaginary cloth.

The first swindler looked up and said, "As you can see, your Majesty, we have nearly completed

our work on your magic garment."

The second swindler added, "We trust you'll find that all is satisfactory. We have to move the buttons a bit higher to emphasize your Majesty's broad shoulders, but aside from that, Sire . . . "

"Magnificent!" sighed the first minister. "My, but aren't those colors beautiful!"

"Isn't their use of pattern absolutely brilliant?" asked the second minister.

"What's this?" thought the Emperor. "The weavers can see the cloth, my ministers can see it, but I can't see anything! Am I a fool? Am I unfit to be Emperor? This is terrible! What a thing to happen to me, of all people!"

But nothing could make him say that he didn't see anything. Instead, he smiled, made each of the swindlers a knight, and announced that he would wear the new clothes at the great procession soon to take place.

At last came that long-awaited day when the swindlers delivered the Emperor's new clothes! The

Emperor hurried to the throne room to try them on. As he entered the room, both swindlers raised their arms, as though something was draped across them.

"Here is your robe," said the first swindler, pretending to place it upon the Emperor's shoulders. "Lovely, isn't it!"

"Light as spider's silk!" smiled the second swindler. "One would almost think he had nothing on, but that's what makes these garments so fine!"

The ladies-in-waiting agreed with the gentlemen of the court that the entire outfit was magnificent! Happily the Emperor ordered that the weavers each be given a large bag of gold while he retired to his dressing room to put on all his new clothes for the procession.

The swindlers bowed, took their bags of gold, then left quickly.

Soon there came the blare of trumpets. Someone said, "The red carpet for the procession is in place, Sire."

"I am ready," said the Emperor, turning one last time in front of his

mirror, to be certain everything was on just right. This was difficult to do because all the Emperor could see was his underwear.

At last he placed his crown upon his head, his mantle upon his shoulders, and marched at the head of the procession upon the royal red carpet.

All the people who lined the streets and peered from their windows cried, "Just look at the Emperor's new clothes! Aren't they beautiful!" Nobody dared confess that he didn't see anything, for that would prove him unfit for his job, or a fool. Indeed, no costume the Emperor had worn before was ever such a complete success!

Then suddenly a little child cried, "Look! The Emperor has no clothes on!"

At first, there was absolute silence. No one knew what to say. Was their Emperor really wearing no clothes?

Then, one person began to whisper to another about what the

child had said. The Emperor began to blush. An innocent child had said the Emperor was wearing no clothes! It was true.

"He hasn't got anything on!" the whole town cried out at last . . . and they started to laugh.

The Emperor squirmed. He knew that what the people were saying was so.

A minister suggested that the procession return quickly to the castle. The Emperor agreed.

(Had he learned his lesson? Time would tell.)

Jack and the Beanstalk

(An Old English Tale)

Once upon a time in the countryside, a boy named Jack lived with his mother, who was a widow. They owned an old cow and little else, for they were very poor.

Jack was a clever boy who loved to dream that some day he would go out and make his fortune. Then he and his mother would live in great comfort. Meanwhile, there was scarcely a crust of bread in the house. A hard, cold spring had been followed by a dry summer in which the grass in the meadow had withered; so the cow gave no milk to drink or to sell.

One day, Jack's mother sighed wearily and said, "I'm afraid we're going to have to sell the old cow, Jack. There simply isn't enough for us to eat."

"All right, Mother," replied Jack. "I'll sell her and fetch a good price for her, you'll see."

Though Jack knew he and his mother would sorely miss the old cow, he also knew they couldn't afford to feed her a day longer; so he set off for the market far away. Over and over his mother had warned him, "They'll try to cheat you, Jack. Be sure you get a fair price for her!"

Before he had walked very far, Jack met a strange old man tapping his way along with a stick. He looked up as the boy and his cow drew near, then said, "Wait, Jack!" A complete stranger, yet he knew

Jack's name! "Where are you off to on this fine, bright day?" he asked.

"Why, I'm off to the market to sell my cow," Jack replied.

"Oh, indeed," said the old man. "Well, I'll take her. See what you shall have in exchange." The old man opened a wrinkled hand in which he clutched five beans.

"Five beans!" cried Jack. "What kind of exchange do you call that?"

"Ah," said the old man, "but these are no common beans. They're magic beans! Just plant them and they'll grow up to the sky!"

Now Jack had never seen magic beans before, but how was he to know whether the beans were truly magical?

"If the beans aren't all I say," continued the old man, "meet me here tomorrow at this hour and you shall have your cow back again—fair?"

Jack thought that was indeed a fair offer, so he agreed to the exchange. He handed the cow's halter to the old man, begged him to be good to her, then took the beans and ran home.

When he told his mother what

had happened and placed the beans in her hand, she threw them out the window in a rage! "Magic beans, indeed!" she cried. "To trade our only cow for a few beans was stupid, Jack! You were cheated. Now we have no money to buy bread, and no cow to give us milk or butter. Go to bed this instant, you dolt. No supper for you from this night on!"

Upstairs in his little room, Jack lay on his bed and began to think how foolish he had been. Oh, how he had disappointed his poor mother! No wonder she had grown so angry! He ate the crust of bread she had given him, swallowed a sip of water, and soon fell into a troubled sleep.

In the morning, when he awoke, Jack was surprised to see strange, leafy shadows on the walls. At first he thought he must be dreaming. Then, looking toward the window, he saw that it was covered with broad green leaves growing from strong, twisting stems. He leaped from his bed, ran to the window, and stared in disbelief at a gigantic stalk that stretched from the ground below to the clouds above!

"It's a beanstalk!" he gasped. "It reaches to the sky! It must have grown from those beans Mother tossed out the window. Then the old man didn't cheat me! The beans were magic!"

Jack's heart was pounding with excitement! How high did the beanstalk reach? He had to know! He leaped upon the stalk. Seeing that it bore him easily, Jack started to climb. Up, up, up he went, higher and higher, till he could look down and see his mother's cottage far below.

The top of the stalk reached above the clouds. Jack climbed all the way to the top and saw, to his surprise, a strange house looming in the distance. He stepped off the beanstalk onto the clouds and began walking cautiously toward the house. When he came close, he realized that the house was much taller than any he had ever seen on earth.

"I wonder who lives here?" he thought. "The doors to this house are gigantic!" Jack had eaten no breakfast and his climb up the beanstalk had sharpened his appetite. Discovering one of the doors

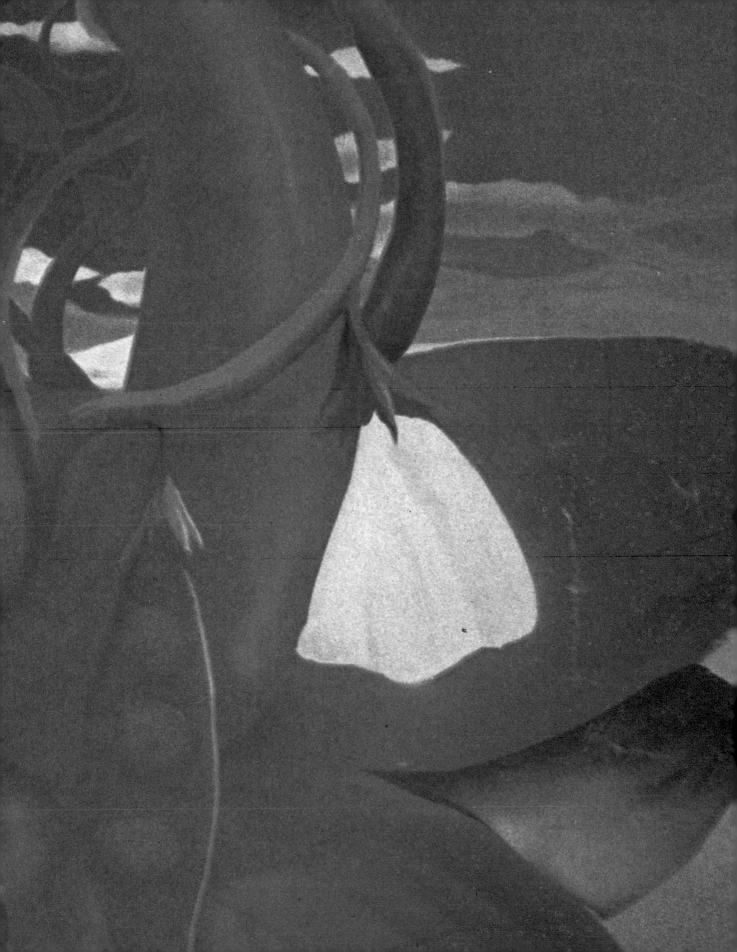

ajar, he crept into the strange house, found his way to the kitchen, and began looking for something to eat. What he found, instead, was a gigantic table upon which lay a pile of bones that had been picked bare.

Suddenly there came a terrible noise and the house began to shake. Thump! Thump! Thump! Something huge was coming into the house! Jack hid in the fireplace.

Into the kitchen stomped a creature such as Jack had never seen—a giant ogre! "So that's why this house is so tall!" thought Jack. The giant looked all around the kitchen. He began sniffing and snuffing the air. Then he said, in a voice that shook the kettles in the fireplace,

"Fee, fie, foh, fum!
I smell the blood of an English-
  man.
Be he alive, or be he dead,
I'll grind his bones to make my
  bread!"

"If he finds me here," thought Jack, "it's the end of me!"

The giant sniffed his way toward the fireplace where Jack was hiding. The boy cringed in fear! Then the ogre lifted a bone from the kettle over Jack's head and muttered, "Hmph! Must be the scent of that traveler I cooked last night."

The ogre went to a big iron chest against the wall and removed three bags of gold. He emptied them on the table, counted the golden coins, then put the coins back in the bags and soon fell happily asleep. The ogre's snores sounded like thunder!

Jack crept out of the fireplace, gently lifted a bag of gold from the table, tiptoed back outside the house, then ran as fast as he could till he came to the beanstalk. Down he clambered! A short time later, he was back on the ground.

"Well, Mother," laughed Jack as he emptied the bag on her table, "what do you think of your stupid son now?" His mother, dazzled by the sight of so many shiny golden coins, had to admit that Jack was as clever as she had always known he was, and that the beans were not such a bad bargain at that.

For a long time they lived in comfort and happiness, spending the gold coins for meat and drink and many new things they had wanted for so long.

But even a bag of gold does not last forever. The day came when the last gold coin was spent. The moneybag was empty. Then Jack's thoughts turned once again to the beanstalk. "It can't be helped," he said to himself. "It's dangerous, but I've got to climb the beanstalk again and this time do even better."

So once again he climbed the beanstalk, up, up, up, till at last he set foot upon the clouds. Carefully he made his way to the ogre's house where, seeing no one, he slipped inside and tiptoed toward the big iron chest in the kitchen where the giant kept his bags of gold.

Suddenly the whole house shook! Thump! Thump! Thump! Without so much as a thought, Jack ran into the fireplace and hid as the giant stomped into the kitchen. Again the ogre sniffed and snuffed the air.

"Fee, fie, foh, fum!
I smell the blood of an Englishman!
Be he alive or be he dead,
I'll grind his bones to make my bread!"

And again he followed his nose right to the fireplace where Jack remained hidden, trembling with fear. The ogre lifted the lid of a kettle hanging over Jack's head. "Hm," he muttered, "must be the scent of those two fat boys I cooked for breakfast." He replaced the lid on the kettle, then brought in a fine

hen. Jack was afraid the ogre planned to roast the hen in the fireplace! But this was no ordinary hen.

The ogre sat at the table, placed the pretty little hen in front of him, and said, "Lay!" The hen immediately laid an egg of pure gold!

Peeking from inside the fireplace, Jack rubbed his eyes at the sight. "A golden egg!" he whispered to himself. "What wouldn't Mother give to see that!"

"Lay!" the ogre commanded, and the hen laid another golden egg. "Lay! . . . Lay! . . . Lay!" said the giant—and each time the magic hen laid an egg of purest gold.

After a while, the giant tired of this. He yawned mightily. When Jack heard snores as loud as thunder, he knew the giant was sound asleep and he crept out of his hiding place. He tiptoed to the table, gently lifted the hen, then ran out of the house. The running alarmed the hen. It began to cackle, but by now Jack was far enough away so that the noise did not disturb the snoring giant. Down the beanstalk clambered the boy, with the hen tucked safely under his arm.

"Look, Mother!" he soon was saying, barely able to contain his excitement. "This is no common hen. Watch." He set the hen upon his mother's table. "Lay!" he commanded. The hen laid a golden egg. The boy's mother gasped, as he knew she would. "Lay! . . . Lay! . . . Lay!" Each time the hen laid an egg of purest gold!

The widow was amazed at the cleverness of her son. She knew that—with a magic hen which laid golden eggs upon command—there was no need for Jack ever to climb the beanstalk again.

But Jack, prosperous and happy once more, soon grew restless. He wondered what other treasures the ogre might have. So one fine morning, yearning for a bit of excitement, he climbed the beanstalk again, made his way to the ogre's house, and hid in the kitchen fireplace just as the house began to shake!

Thump! Thump! Thump!

The ogre entered the kitchen, then suddenly stopped. He sniffed and snuffed the air.

"Fee fie, foh, fum!
I smell the blood of an Englishman!
Be he alive or be he dead,
I'll grind his bones to make my bread!"

The ogre, who had already lost a bag of gold and his magic hen to a thief, searched everywhere. He looked in the kettles that hung in the fireplace, but he never thought of looking under the kettles. "Hm," he said at last, "I could have sworn I smelled a boy."

He sat down wearily at his table

and placed before him a little golden harp. "Sing, harp," he said; and the magic harp started playing and singing all by itself! Strange were the songs it sang, but so beautiful that Jack nearly started singing them, too!

After a while the ogre fell asleep. Jack crept out of the fireplace, tiptoed to the table, and lifted the magic harp. No sooner had he done so than the harp struck a loud, crashing chord and cried, "Help, Master, help!"

The ogre, sleeping only lightly because he suspected something awry from the start, opened his eyes just in time to see Jack running out of the house! He leaped to his feet and started after the boy!

Jack ran through the clouds faster than he had ever run before! The ogre, fortunately for Jack, fell over a step in his haste to rush out of the house. Cursing and swearing, he picked himself up and bounded after the boy again, each of his steps equaling ten of Jack's!

"Help, Master, help!" the harp kept crying. Jack reached the beanstalk not a moment too soon! Not even taking the time to clamber down quickly, he almost slid down and, in so doing, nearly fell off the beanstalk, high above the ground!

Halfway down, the stalk began to tremble and shake violently! Jack looked up and saw that the ogre had leaped onto it and was sliding down after him! The stalk tottered and swayed under the giant's weight; it was all Jack could do to hold on for his life!

Near the bottom, Jack called, "Mother! Mother, the ax! Get the ax!" The widow heard her son shouting and by the time he set foot on the ground, she was there waiting for him, ax in hand. He grabbed the ax and swung at the beanstalk with all his might. Whack! The ax slashed nearly halfway through the pulpy stalk. Whack! The ax cut past the halfway mark.

Suddenly a great, dark shadow covered the ground. The ogre was coming closer and closer! Jack gritted his teeth and with all the

remaining strength he could summon, swung again with the ax! Whack!

This time the ax cut right through the stalk! The mighty plant shook and trembled, then it toppled to earth with the giant ogre clinging to its side! A roar was heard in towns far away as the great beanstalk crashed to the ground with such force that it created a huge hole and sent a cloud of dust flying high into the air!

When the dust settled, not a trace of the ogre could be seen.

From that day on, Jack was content to remain quietly at home with his mother. With their magic hen providing all the gold they would ever need, and their magic harp delighting them with songs strange and beautiful, they lived happily ever after.

Hansel and Gretel

(The Brothers Grimm, Germany)

Once upon a time, at the edge of a great forest, there stood a cabin that belonged to a poor woodcutter. He lived with his two children—a boy and a girl whom he dearly loved—and with the children's stepmother, who had no love for the children at all!

One night, the boy, Hansel, tried to awaken his sister, Gretel. He could overhear his father and stepmother speaking about how little food there was to eat.

"What's to become of us?" whispered the poor woodcutter. "We had little enough to eat before. Now, with this famine in our land, how are we going to feed the children? We no longer have enough for ourselves."

"Listen to me," replied his wife.

"Tomorrow we will take both children into the wildest part of the forest and give each one a bit of bread. Then we will return home and leave them there—for good!"

The woodcutter was saddened by the idea, but he agreed there was no choice. Gretel began to weep softly. Hansel gently put his arm around her and said, "Don't worry, Gretel. We'll be able to find our way back. I have a plan."

Early the next morning, before anyone else was awake, Hansel stole out to the clearing surrounding the cabin, where many shiny pebbles sparkled in the first rays of the sun. One by one, Hansel gathered the pebbles and began stuffing them into his pockets! Suddenly, he was startled by the harsh voice

of his stepmother calling from the cabin. "Hansel!"

"Yes?" he replied, fearing that his plan had been discovered.

"What are you doing out there?"

"Oh . . . nothing . . . "

"Wake up your lazy sister!" snapped the boy's stepmother. "We're going to fetch firewood!"

Hansel breathed a sign of relief. The woman had not seen him stuffing the shiny pebbles into his pockets.

Soon the woodcutter, his wife, and the two children set out together into the forest. As they walked, Hansel secretly dropped one shiny pebble after another along the path.

Later, as the sound of the woodcutter's ax echoed through the middle of the forest, Hansel and Gretel played happily. They had eaten their little bit of bread and now were alone. As evening approached, they decided they had better look for their father. They walked through the woods toward the place where they heard the sound of the woodcutter's ax.

When they reached that spot, though, they saw to their surprise that the sound was not made by an ax at all, but by a branch that the woodcutter's wife had tied to a dead tree! All day long the wind had blown it to and fro!

Gretel grew frightened and began to cry. She wondered how they'd ever get out of the forest. Hansel comforted her. "Don't cry, Gretel," he said. "When the moon comes out, we'll find our way back home."

The sky grew darker and darker. Then, little by little, the moon began to rise above the treetops. As it rose ever higher, silvery moonbeams began to dance upon the shiny pebbles Hansel had dropped along the path. The pebbles glistened like newly minted silver coins.

Happily, Hansel took his little sister by the hand and followed the pebbles that pointed the way. Soon they were out of the forest and racing along a familiar ledge that led to home!

The children's father, who had worried about them from the start,

was the first to hear them coming! He ran to the door of his cabin and threw it open just as Hansel and Gretel were about to open it themselves. "Hansel! Gretel!" he laughed, scooping the children into his arms. "Father! Father!" the children cried, hugging and kissing him. All were happy . . . except the woodcutter's wife! She scowled and made up her mind once again to get rid of the children.

Early the next morning, she awakened them, but gave Hansel no time to go out and gather pebbles. She said they were leaving immediately for a picnic in the woods. Her plan was to take the children even deeper into the forest . . . then leave them there!

This time, having no pebbles, Hansel broke off crumbs from the small piece of bread he had received and dropped them along the path. But as he did so, small birds were following close behind, eating the crumbs!

That night, the children found themselves alone in a strange part of the forest. The woodcutter and his wife were nowhere in sight, and the children understood that their stepmother had once again made their father agree to leave them behind.

Again the children waited for the moon to rise, thinking they would then be able to see the bread crumbs Hansel had dropped. But when the moon rose, not a single bread crumb was to be seen.

Hansel searched and searched in vain, then finally said, "The bread crumbs I dropped to mark the path are gone."

"Now we'll never be able to find our way home!" sobbed Gretel.

"Yes, we will, Gretel," said Hansel, trying to be brave. "We'll get out of the forest somehow."

Hand in hand, they began walking through the forest, their shadows casting frightening shapes on gnarled old trees. Everything looked frightening at night. Strange eyes peered at them from the darkness. Strange sounds pierced the air. Cautiously the children made their way. They dared not stop! On and on they trudged . . . all night long and into the next day.

Then, as evening approached, Gretel—who could scarcely take

another step—suddenly stopped and gasped, "Hansel! Look!" She pointed to a clearing in the forest. "Is that a house?"

There was something in the clearing, to be sure, but its shape was so strange that Hansel couldn't tell exactly what it was. "Let's go and see," he said.

Tired as they were, the children ran to the clearing where the strange shape rose. It was a house—a house such as they had never seen! It was made of gingerbread and cake! The walls and roof were covered with whipped cream and candy! The door was made of spun sugar! Lemonade leaped from a fountain! Hansel and Gretel were so hungry that Hansel broke off a bit of the roof to eat, while Gretel plucked a giant lollipop!

Suddenly a rasping voice asked, "Is that a mouse who eats my house?"

Startled, the children turned to see an old woman standing at an open window. "We're awfully sorry," said Hansel. "We didn't mean to eat your house, but we were so hungry——"

"Oh, poor dears," the old woman

said with a sigh. "All alone in the forest? Please, come in and have pancakes and honey with me."

The children were both relieved and happy. "Why, thank you! We'd love to!" said Hansel. Gretel smiled at the old woman. "You're very kind," she said.

But the old woman was only pretending to be kind. Had Hansel and Gretel looked closely at her, they'd have noticed that the old woman had ruby red eyes, showing that she was really a wicked witch—a witch who lay in wait for children!

That night, as the boy and his sister slept, the witch walked over and looked at them. "Ha! They're all alike," she thought. "They can't resist this house. In the morning, I'll toss the boy into the cage and start fattening him up. He'll make a tasty morsel!"

The next morning, when Hansel least expected it, the old woman grabbed him, shoved him into a dark little cage, and slammed the gate shut behind him! Now the children knew the old woman was a witch. But it was too late!

Gretel was put to work and or-

dered to do whatever was necessary to fatten up her brother. The poor girl wept silent tears . . . in vain. Each day she had to cook big pots of fattening food for Hansel.

Each morning the witch went to the cage and said, "Hansel, stick out your finger so I can tell how fat you're getting." But instead, the clever boy stuck out a bone, knowing that those red eyes of the witch saw very little, indeed. "I simply can't understand it!" cried the witch. "You're still as skinny as a bone!"

After four weeks of this, the witch's patience was exhausted. "I won't wait another day," she thought. Then she turned to Gretel and called, "Make a fire in the oven! We're going to bake bread!"

Gretel started a fire in the oven, tears spilling down her cheeks, for she knew the witch was planning not to bake bread, but her brother and her!

"Now," said the witch, "stick your head in the oven and see if it's hot enough to bake bread."

"I don't know how to do it," replied Gretel. "But if you'll show me . . ."

"Stupid goose!" shouted the witch. "It's easy enough." She opened the oven door and stuck her head inside. "Just put your head way in, like this. See?"

Gretel saw very well. She gave the witch a push, shoving her all the way in, slammed the oven door shut behind her, and ran to let Hansel out of his cage.

"Oh! Oh!" cried the witch, deep inside the oven. "Dreadful child! What have you done? I'm melting!" That was the end of her!

Hansel, out of the cage, threw his arms around Gretel and the children hopped and skipped for joy. Then, quick as they could, they ran from the witch's cottage toward the warm sunshine!

Soon they reached a wide stream with no bridge across it. But a helpful swan told them that, if they would climb on his back, he would take them where they wanted to go.

The swan carried them far downstream to a spot on the other shore where a neat little path ran near the water's edge. The children thanked the swan, set out upon the path and—almost before they

knew it—found themselves approaching the familiar ledge near their house!

Imagine how happy they were, after weeks away, to be home!

Their father, who had been grieving for his lost children all this time, was sitting in front of the hearth, gazing sadly into the fire. Suddenly the door burst open and in ran Hansel and Gretel!

The poor woodcutter's eyes filled with tears of joy. He gathered his children into his arms and kissed them over and over!

When Hansel and Gretel noticed that their stepmother was nowhere in sight, the woodcutter explained, "Your stepmother died last week, children. We three will never be separated again!"

And, indeed, Hansel and Gretel and their good father lived happily ever after.

The Wolf and the Seven Kids

(The Brothers Grimm, Germany)

Once upon a time, at the edge of a green meadow, there stood a house made of stone. In the house lived a mother goat and her seven children. The little goats, or "kids," loved to spend their days frolicking in the meadow.

If one was hurt, Mother Goat would dry its tears and do everything a good mother does for her children. For she loved them very much. And they loved her. They were happy living together in the meadow.

But in the woods nearby roamed a hungry wolf who lived on small animals!

One fine morning, Mother Goat gathered her seven little ones around her and said, "Listen carefully, children. I must go out shopping. While I'm out, you must not permit anyone to come into the house, understand? The wolf may come and try to pretend he's someone else, but you can recognize him right away by his gruff voice and dark paws."

"Don't worry, Mother," said the kids. "We won't let him in." Mother Goat left, satisfied that the kids would remember her warning. The wolf, hiding behind a tree, saw her go!

Soon after, he knocked on the door! "Open the door, children," he called in his sweetest voice. "This is Mother. I'm back, and I brought each of you a present!"

The seven kids laughed. They knew that gruff voice belonged to the wolf!

"What are you laughing about? Come open the door," said the wolf, still in his sweetest voice.

"We won't!" replied the kids. "You're not Mother. Mother's voice is soft, but yours is gruff. You are the wolf!"

The wolf gnashed his teeth in anger, then ran to a drugstore and demanded some medicine that would soothe his gruff voice. He drank the medicine in one gulp. It made his voice soft. Then he ran back and once again knocked on the goats' door!

"Open the door, dear children," he called sweetly. "It's Mother. I'm back, and I brought each of you a present."

"Mother?" asked the seven kids.

"Yes. It's quite safe to open the door now, my dears. The wolf has gone away."

But the kids peeked under the door and saw the wolf's dark paws. "We won't open the door!" they cried. "Our mother doesn't have dark paws. You are the wolf!"

The wolf gnashed his teeth in anger. This time, he ran to a baker

and made the poor man sprinkle flour on his paws, till they were white.

"Perfect!" laughed the wolf. "Now, with a soft voice and white feet, those kids will surely think I am Mother Goat!"

He went to the door a third time, knocked, and said, "Open the door. It's your mother, children. I'm home from shopping and I've brought each of you a present!"

The kids peeked under the door and saw paws that were white as milk. "Good! It's really Mother this time!" they laughed . . . and they opened the door!

Imagine their surprise when they saw the wolf! Terrified, the kids fled and tried to hide! One leaped under a table, the second crawled into bed, the third hid in the stove, the fourth in the kitchen, the fifth in a cupboard, the sixth beneath a washbasin, the seventh in the cabinet of a grandfather clock!

But, one by one, the wolf found them and gulped them down—except for the youngest hiding in the clock. That one he missed. The

wolf's hunger was satisfied. With stomach swollen till it nearly burst, he strolled into the meadow, stretched out under a tree, and went happily to sleep.

Soon afterward, Mother Goat returned. What a sight greeted her! The door was wide open! The table, chairs, and benches were overturned! The washbasin lay shattered in a dozen pieces! Covers and pillows had been yanked off the beds! The entire house was a shambles!

"Oh, my!" thought Mother Goat. "What could have happened?" She searched for her children and called each by name. None replied. The youngest kid, fearing another trick, remained silent at first. Then, peeking out of the clock cabinet, he could see his mother. "Mother!" he called. "I'm in the clock!"

Mother Goat got him out. "Oh, my youngest! My baby!" she cried. "Tell me what happened!"

"The wolf tricked us, Mother," said the youngest kid. He explained how the wolf had entered and eaten all the others.

Imagine how Mother Goat wept

for her poor children! Finally, with her youngest running at her side, she went out to look for the wolf. They crossed the meadow and there they found the wolf stretched out under a tree, sound asleep!

Suddenly, something began stirring and struggling inside his swollen stomach. "The children!" gasped Mother Goat. She told her youngest kid to run home as fast as he could and fetch scissors, needle, and thread! When he returned, Mother Goat leaned over the wolf's stomach, then carefully snipped an opening large enough for the kids

to escape! Out they sprang, one after the other!

How happy they were to see their mother and youngest brother again! They wanted to skip and dance for joy! But Mother Goat said, "Sh! We mustn't wake up the wolf! Now go get some big stones, quickly! We'll fill his stomach with them while he's still asleep."

Hurriedly, the kids hauled several large stones and put them all in the wolf's stomach. Then Mother Goat sewed the opening so carefully that the wolf never noticed a thing! He didn't even move!

When the wolf finally awoke, he could hardly stand. "Those kids," he complained, "are as heavy as stones!" Then, because the stones made him thirsty, he went to the pond for a drink.

When he reached the pond, he bent over to drink. But suddenly the heavy stones moved and pulled him forward. Splash! Into the pond he fell—down, down, down! The stones were so heavy, the wolf quickly settled to the bottom.

When the seven kids, watching from nearby, saw what happened, they danced and sang. "That's the end of the wolf! The end of the wolf! He'll never bother us again!"

Mother Goat and the seven kids returned to their home in the green meadow they loved so well. There they lived happily ever after.

Thumbelina

(Hans Christian Andersen, Denmark)

Once there was a woman who had the greatest longing for a tiny child, but was unable to have one. So she went to a sorceress and said, "I do so long for a tiny child."

"Very well," said the sorceress, "you shall have one. Here is a barleycorn, not the same kind that grows in the farmer's field. Plant it in a flowerpot and see what appears."

The woman did as she was told and soon there appeared a flower with red petals much like those of a tulip. "What a lovely flower!" exclaimed the woman, and she kissed it. At that, the petals snapped open and there, sitting on the tiny green stool in the midst of the flower, was a beautiful girl no bigger than the woman's thumb!

The girl was promptly named Thumbelina. Her cradle was a varnished walnut shell, in which she slept at night. During the day, she played on a table where the woman had set a plate filled with water and surrounded by flowers. Thumbelina floated on the water in a large tulip petal, singing happily with such delicacy as was never heard before.

Then one stormy night, as Thumbelina lay sleeping in her bed, a great ugly toad hopped in at the window through a broken pane. It hopped right onto the table where Thumbelina lay fast asleep!

"What a lovely wife for my son!" thought the toad. She lifted the walnut shell in which Thumbelina was sleeping, hopped back

through the window with it, then down into the garden where a broad stream ran. Here the toad lived with her son, who was just as ugly as his mother.

Thumbelina, still asleep, was placed on a broad water lily far from shore, so she could not escape. When she opened her eyes, she was startled to see the toads staring at her. The old toad curtsied and said, "This is my son. He approves of you, my dear, so now the two of you are to be married and live quite comfortably down in the mud!"

"Croax-croax!" was all the young toad could say.

They took Thumbelina's pretty little bed and swam away with it to put it in a room under the mud, where the young toad and his bride would live. Thumbelina sat alone on the water lily. She started to cry because she did not want to marry the ugly toad and live under the mud.

Little fish swimming in the stream had heard everything. When they saw Thumbelina, they were so delighted with her that they could not bear to think of her living in mud with the toad. So they gnawed at the stem of the leaf beneath her, until soon the leaf was free and Thumbelina was floating downstream, far away from the toads.

She sailed past place after place. Birds saw her and sang sweetly to her. A little butterfly took a fancy to her and fluttered around and around. Then it took hold of her sash and began pulling her toward shore, where she could make her way home.

Suddenly, a huge cockchafer came flying by, saw Thumbelina, and snatched her away! Up, up they went into a tree, where the chafer set her upon a large leaf. He thought she was lovely, although not a bit like a chafer. Other chafers that lived in the tree came to visit and look over the newcomer.

"She has no feelers!" exclaimed one lady cockchafer.

"Too slender in the waist!" complained another.

"Fie!" cried a third. "She's ugly! She looks like a human being!"

When all the others agreed she was ugly, the cockchafer that captured Thumbelina began to believe

it, too, and wished nothing more to do with her. He flew down from the tree with her and dropped her upon a daisy.

Poor Thumbelina lived all summer alone in the wood. Her food was honey from the flowers; her drink was dew from the leaves. But soon autumn came. Then winter. Birds that used to sing to her so sweetly flew away. The flowers in which she lived shriveled and died. Snow began to fall; each snowflake struck her as a whole shovelful would upon one of us, since she was so tiny.

Thumbelina, trembling with the cold, wrapped herself in a withered leaf that did little to warm her, and began trudging through the snow. Nearby lay a large cornfield, but the corn had been picked long ago. The poor girl had not eaten for two days. Then she came to the door of a field mouse's home.

"Poor thing," said the kind field mouse. She took an immediate liking to Thumbelina. "Come into my warm room and dine with me. Stay the winter, if you wish, for there is more than enough for us both to eat. All you must do is keep the

room clean and tidy and tell me stories. I am very fond of stories."

Thumbelina did as she was bid and was soon quite comfortable. Then the field mouse said, "Soon we shall have a visitor. My neighbor comes to see me regularly. He must be very rich, for he wears a fine black coat and has a house twenty times as large as mine. If you could get him for a husband, you would be well settled, indeed. But he cannot see. You must entertain him, my dear."

Soon the neighbor came to visit in his fine black coat. He was a mole. Thumbelina sang for him, but did not like the mole at all, for he disliked the sun and beautiful flowers; in fact, he spoke poorly of them, as he had never seen them. The mole, however, fell in love with Thumbelina's sweet, delicate voice. He invited her and the field mouse to see a new tunnel he had just dug.

He walked in front of them, lighting the way through the long, dark tunnel. Suddenly he thrust his broad nose up to the roof and poked aside the earth, making a hole through which daylight en-

tered. "I did that so you could see the dead bird in the way," he said. "It died of the cold, no doubt." On the floor lay a swallow, its wings pressed closely to its sides. The mole kicked it with his short legs and said, "Thank heaven no child of mine can be a bird! All they do is twitter in the summer, then die of hunger in the winter." The field mouse agreed.

Thumbelina said nothing, but thought, "This may be one of the dear birds that sang to me so sweetly last summer." That night,

she could not sleep. She crept from her bed and made a mat of hay which she carried to the bird and covered him with it, so that he might have a warm bed. Then she laid her head upon the bird's breast. Suddenly, she was startled by a thumping sound inside it! It was the bird's heart! He was alive! The warmth had revived him!

Thumbelina went outside, covered the hole in the roof with dried leaves to keep out the cold wind, then scooped up snow that would melt into water for the swallow to drink. Beneath the snow she found seeds for the bird to eat. All through the winter she nursed the bird, but told neither the field mouse nor the mole about it. When he could speak again, the sick swallow explained that he had injured his wing on a thorn bush and fallen behind the flock as it migrated to warm, distant lands. At last, he had fallen to the ground, but after that remembered nothing.

By the time spring came, the swallow had regained its strength. "Sweet Thumbelina," he said, "climb on my back and we'll fly far away into the green wood!" But Thumbelina knew the old field mouse would grieve if she were suddenly left alone like that.

"No, I can't," said Thumbelina, "I must stay."

"Goodbye, then, you kind, pretty girl," said the swallow, and he flew out the hole in the roof into the warm sunshine. "Thank you!" he called.

"Goodbye!" said Thumbelina, her eyes filled with tears. She had grown very fond of the swallow.

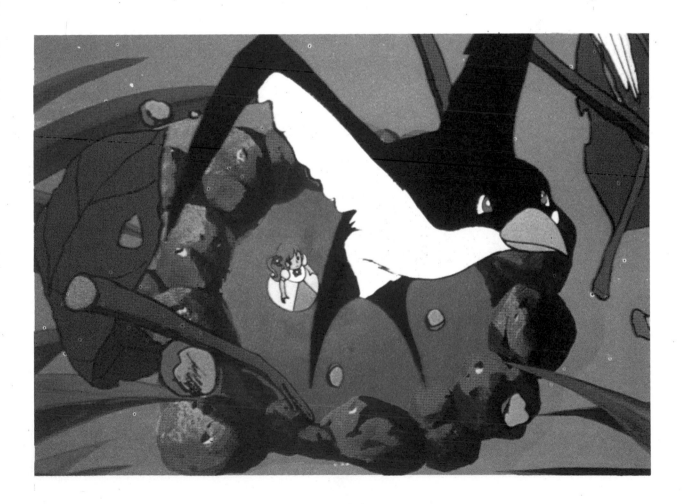

Soon after, the tiresome mole in his fine black coat said he wanted to marry Thumbelina. The field mouse thought that was a splendid idea! But Thumbelina cried and said she would not have a tiresome mole for a husband.

"Fiddlesticks!" snapped the field mouse. "You should be thankful to have such a fine, rich husband as the mole! When the summer has come to an end, and the sun no longer bakes the ground as hard as rock, your wedding gown must be finished and you shall be married to the mole!"

Thumbelina had to work at her trousseau all summer long. The field mouse hired four spiders to spin and weave day and night. The mole came to visit every morning.

By autumn, Thumbelina's outfit was ready. The mole in his black coat came to fetch Thumbelina. She was to live deep under the ground with him, never to go out into the bright sunshine, for he could not bear it. The poor child was sad at the thought of bidding goodbye to the sun. She opened the door, walked a little way from the field mouse's house, stood in

the sunshine for what was to be the
last time, and said "Goodbye,
bright sun."

Just then, she heard a loud
"Tweet! Tweet!" She looked up. It
was the swallow! He had been flying by when he saw Thumbelina.
She told him all that had happened
and could not help crying about it.

"Winter is coming," said the
swallow. "Come, fly away with me
to the warm countries, far from the
ugly mole and his dark caves!"

"Yes," said Thumbelina. "This
time I will go with you."

The field mouse appeared in the

open doorway, looking for the
bride-to-be. "Thumbelina!" she
called.

"Dearest friend," replied the tiny
girl, "you've been so kind. I don't
want to leave. But I cannot marry
the mole and live underground, so
I'm flying away with the swallow."

"Thumbelina! Come back!" cried
the field mouse, running toward
the child as fast as she could. But
Thumbelina was already upon the
swallow's back. Away they flew,
high into the air!

Soon they were passing over
forests and lakes, soaring above

high mountains where snow never melts, till at last they reached the warm countries. Then the swallow flew down into a lovely green field covered with dazzling flowers, and set Thumbelina upon a velvety white petal.

Imagine her astonishment to discover a tiny young man in the midst of the flower! He was no bigger than she and he wore a golden crown. Tiny, beautiful women and men appeared in every flower, but he was clearly the king of them all.

When he saw Thumbelina, he was delighted; she was the pret-tiest girl he had ever seen. "Welcome home, Thumbelina!" he said. "I am the King of the flowers. This is your true home and we've all been waiting for you."

Then Thumbelina understood. In each flower lives a tiny angel. She had come from a flower; she, too, was an angel! The king had fallen in love with her the moment he saw her; and she with him.

He took the golden crown from his head, placed it on hers, and asked if she would be his wife. What a different kind of husband from the toad . . . or the mole with

his black coat! Thumbelina accepted.

Now it was time for the swallow to leave. "Goodbye, goodbye!" he called.

"Goodbye, dear swallow," called Thumbelina.

The swallow left with a heavy heart. He had grown fond of Thumbelina himself, and would have wished never to part from her. But he knew this is where she was meant to be. She was meant to be Queen of the Flowers!

Aladdin and the Wonderful Lamp

Once upon a time, long long ago, when the ancient city of Baghdad was still new, a boy named Aladdin lived with his mother, who was a poor widow. Aladdin was an idle boy who did little to help his mother. Much of his time was spent in the marketplace wandering aimlessly among stalls with boys from the gutter. For amusement, they would annoy the merchants—tease them, fight with them, and sometimes even damage their stalls.

Time after time, merchants came to see Aladdin's mother, demanding to be paid for damages. "Your son has wrecked our stalls!" they shouted. "We must be repaid!"

Aladdin's mother would weep. She had fallen to spinning cotton yarn after her husband died. There was little enough money to buy food, let alone pay for her son's mischief. Then, one day, a swarthy stranger stepped forward from behind a group of angry merchants.

"Enough!" he shouted. "I am Maglev. I shall pay for all damages done by Aladdin!"

The stranger later explained to Aladdin's mother that he was the brother of her poor dead husband. Yes, he was Aladdin's uncle, he said. He had been away, trading in distant lands for forty years. Now he had returned to his own land to rest and be a good uncle to his poor brother's son. Maglev said he felt like a father to the boy already and seemed surpised to hear that Aladdin, who had reached his fifteenth year, had no trade. "Why, then," he smiled, "I shall gladly teach Aladdin the art of trading with distant lands!"

Now, Aladdin's mother had doubted that the stranger was her dead husband's brother. She had never heard of this brother before. But when she heard him promise to pay for Aladdin's damages and to teach her son the art of trading with other lands, she concluded that this swarthy stranger must indeed be her husband's brother. So she bade Aladdin to obey his good uncle.

Aladdin was happy. Becoming a merchant, buying and selling, trading, being known far and wide—all this appealed to him. And he would learn it from a master, his very own uncle.

But in truth, Maglev was not Aladdin's uncle at all. He was a sorcerer from Africa who saw in Aladdin a boy with the very qualities he had been seeking.

Early next morning, he knocked at the door and asked Aladdin to join him on a short journey to a bazaar beyond the city gate. The boy's apprenticeship was to begin

at once! Aladdin was delighted to be traveling so far from home, seeing sights and wonders such as he had never seen! But when at last the city had fallen far behind them and the bazaar was still nowhere in sight, Aladdin asked, "Uncle, where are we going? There is no bazaar before us. It will soon be dark and we should return to town."

By now, they had reached the base of a high, rocky hill. "Patience, my son!" cautioned Maglev. "I will show you a rare and beauti-ful sight." The sorcerer waved his hands at a huge rock at the base of the hill and shouted, "Shahzad!" A burst of green smoke and flame flashed from the rock and suddenly the mighty rock rumbled into place high above the ground!

Aladdin gaped at the sight. Where the rock had stood there now appeared a dark cave in which a stairway carved of stone led to a deep underground chamber. "Now, Aladdin," Maglev smiled, "that chamber is the first of four in which great treasures are stored.

At the end of the fourth chamber is an ancient lamp. Bring me the lamp and then we shall return to the city."

But Aladdin was reluctant to enter the cave. This made the sorcerer angry, though he smiled all the more and said, "Ah, clever boy, how wise you are to be cautious. No harm will come to you if you touch only the lamp. Touch nothing else, or you will die instantly." With that he removed a ring and placed it on Aladdin's forefinger.

"This signet," he said, "will protect you. Now bring me the lamp."

When Aladdin still hesitated, Maglev shoved him down the steps. The boy fell to the bottom! Picking himself up, he found himself at the entrance to the first chamber, a chamber not dark at all, but bathed in a warm, ruddy glow. Aladdin was so surprised, he forgot all about himself and began looking around the chamber. The flow came from mounds of copper treasure heaped all around. Alad-

din wanted to feel an ornate copper candlestick, but thought, "Better not. Uncle said I would die instantly." In the next chamber he discovered a treasure in silver and, in the third chamber, several bags of gold. At the end of the fourth chamber, which was darker than the other three, Aladdin could barely make out what appeared to be an ancient lamp. "That must be it," he thought. He took it and began walking back.

Outside the cave, Maglev was growing restless. "A thousand curses upon the young fool!" he muttered. "I alone know where the lamp is hidden—that wonderful lamp that will make me the most powerful man in the world!—yet I can receive it only from the hand of another. Well, when he hands me the lamp, I shall reward him by sealing him in the cave . . . forever!"

Just then came the sound of footsteps on the stairway. "Aladdin?" called the sorcerer.

"Yes, Uncle. These steps are steep and difficult to climb."

"Toss the lamp to me to lighten your load," said Maglev. "Then I'll help you up the steps."

"I'll give you the lamp," Aladdin promised, "but first tell me why you're so eager to have it, and why you shoved me down the steps to get it!"

"Never mind that. Just give me the lamp."

"Not till you give me the answers to both questions!"

Again and again the sorcerer demanded the lamp. At last, when he saw that Aladdin would not hand it over, he grew terribly angry and shouted "Shahzad!" In a burst of green smoke and flame, the huge rock poised high above the ground thundered back into place, sealing the opening to the cave! Aladdin was trapped within!

For two days, the boy roamed from chamber to chamber, crying and lamenting. Then, certain that he would never again set foot outside the cave, he clasped his hands in prayer. "Look after my poor mother," he prayed, "for she has no one to take care of her." In his grief, he rubbed the ring Maglev had given him.

And behold! Before him arose a great Jinni who cried, "What wouldst thou with me? I am the Slave of the Ring and will obey thee in all things. Thy wish is my command, O Master!"

Aladdin trembled at the frightening sight. Then, remembering the sorcerer's words, he grew brave. "Well," he said at last, "I wish I were out of this cave and back home with my mother." No sooner spoken than done! In a twinkling,

the boy was home with his mother. They laughed and cried and he told her all that had happened.

"Now I will sell this ancient lamp," he said. "It will bring more money than your spinning."

"But it is so dirty," said his mother. "If we polish it, it will sell better." Aladdin agreed and started to rub one spot on the lamp. Suddenly there came a great rush of wind! A Jinni arose, larger and more frightening than the Slave of the Ring! The wind died and the Jinni called, "Greetings, my Mas-

ter! I am the all-powerful Slave of the Lamp! What is thy command?"

Aladdin, by now feeling accustomed to commanding Jinn, calmly said, "I'd like my mother to live comfortably. Bring us gold!" No sooner spoken than done! A shower of gold coins filled the room and the Jinni disappeared.

"We must tell no one of this, Mother," Aladdin warned. "We will keep the lamp and guard it well. The same is true of the ring. I will never take it from my finger!"

With his new wealth, Aladdin went to the marketplace. One by one, he repaid the merchants for all the damage he had done in the past; for Maglev had neither kept his promise to pay nor had he been seen ever since.

Then, as Aladdin was returning home, the Sultan's young daughter was being borne through the streets on her way to the palace. To gaze upon her face was forbidden; yet Aladdin longed to see this princess whose beauty was celebrated throughout the land. When she passed, Aladdin pretended to

lower his eyes, but nonetheless he saw her for a fleeting moment. Her loveliness and beauty shone even behind her veil!

From that moment Aladdin was stricken with love for the princess. He went home dazed, raving about her beauty, and vowing one day to marry her! He pleaded with his mother to go to the Sultan to ask permission for the marriage!

"Have you lost your senses?" demanded the boy's mother. "Have you forgotten who you are? How does the son of a widow, the poorest in the city, dare to ask the Sultan for the hand of the princess?"

Aladdin rubbed the wonderful lamp and commanded the Jinni to bring him a bowl of the costliest gems in the world. No sooner spoken than done! "Take this as a gift to the Sultan, Mother," the boy pleaded. "It is an offering whose equal no king possesses."

And so the widow went fearfully to the palace, where she was brought before the Sultan. She bowed and kissed the floor upon which the Sultan walked and said, "O King of Kings, my son Aladdin has fallen in love with the princess and wishes to marry her! I have tried to drive the fancy from his mind, but cannot. I pray you, forgive this boldness!"

The Sultan looked at her kindly, then laughed. "'Tis a most worthy ambition for a poor boy of the streets, to be sure, but how can such a boy support the princess?"

"He sends you this gift," said the boy's mother. She placed the bowl of jewels before him. The Sultan blinked his eyes, dazzled by the brilliant sparkle of the precious gems. "Why, indeed," he said at last, "it is a fitting gift. Who so values her at so great a price deserves to become the bridegroom of my daughter!"

And so it came to pass that Aladdin, a boy of the gutter only a short time before, married the beautiful princess. She fell in love with him as quickly as he had with her. Not far from the Sultan's palace, Aladdin ordered the Jinni to build him a palace befitting the princess; it proved to be a world's wonder! Never were a boy and a girl happier.

Then one day, while Aladdin was away, a swarthy peddler appeared outside the palace. Maglev! He knew that this splendid palace was the work of the all-powerful Jinni and had brought with him several shiny new copper lamps. "New lamps for old, my Masters, new lamps for old," he cried. "Who will trade an old lamp for a new one?"

The princess and her handmaiden, hearing the cry, laughed at the foolishness of the old peddler. The princess knew that Aladdin kept an old lamp, but knew nothing of its magic power. So she sent her handmaiden down to exchange the old lamp. When the maid returned with a new one, they laughed again.

But the sorcerer recognized the wonderful lamp at once! He rubbed it and the Jinni appeared. "Lift this palace with everything in it," commanded Maglev, "and set it down in my gardens in Africa!"

"To hear is to obey," said the Jinni. And in a twinkling it was done.

When Aladdin returned, he was amazed to find not the faintest trace of a building. The Sultan was in tears; his daughter—his only child—had disappeared. Distressed, he gave Aladdin forty days to bring back the princess—or lose his head!

For three days Aladdin wandered about the land, asking everyone what had become of his palace. They only laughed and pitied him. At last he came to a river. In his grief, he thought of throwing himself in, and clasped his hands in prayer. He rubbed the ring, and lo! its Slave appeared. "What wouldst thou of me, O Master?"

Aladdin's heart gladdened. "Slave of the Ring," he called, "take me to my palace, wherever it may be!" In a twinkling the Slave and Aladdin were flying through the air to Africa! Then, just as suddenly, Aladdin found himself scaling the walls of the palace outside the princess' window. In a moment, he had found her and the two embraced each other. They wept with joy.

Maglev had told the princess that Aladdin, powerless without the wonderful lamp, had been be-

headed by the Sultan for the disappearance of his daughter. Now the sorcerer was asking for the hand of the princess in marriage . . . and had gone to bring wine for the wedding ceremony. The princess, who disliked the sight of Maglev, grew sad at the very thought.

"Tell me," Aladdin said, "where does he keep the lamp?"

"He trusts no one and always carries it about with him," the princess replied.

"Very well," said Aladdin. "Tonight, tell him you will marry him.

Gladly. I will arrange a surprise."

That night, the princess adorned herself and when Maglev returned, she welcomed him with a smile. While they ate and drank together, the princess secretly slipped into the sorcerer's wine three drops of a sleeping potion Aladdin had obtained from the Slave of the Ring. Maglev began to grow drowsy.

Then the princess said, "Maglev, I've been considering the marriage. Since Aladdin is dead, and my tears can't bring him back, I will marry you."

Maglev leaped to his feet with delight! "Princess," he laughed, "you've made me the happiest man in the world!" He raised his glass to his lips and quaffed the last drop of wine!

Aladdin had been watching everything from behind a curtain. He knew that by now an ordinary man would have been drugged asleep by the potion in the wine; but the sorcerer was no ordinary man. When he moved to embrace the princess, Aladdin charged into the room, a sword in his hand.

"Maglev!" he called. "I've come for the lamp!"

As drowsy as he was, Maglev removed his own sword and lunged at Aladdin. They duelled back and forth, back and forth, across the room, first the sorcerer gaining the advantage, then the boy. At last, the boy proved to be too much for his opponent. Aladdin's sword found its mark and the sorcerer slumped to the floor, dead.

Aladdin removed the lamp from around Maglev's neck where the

sorcerer kept it on a chain. He summoned the Jinni and ordered, "Take this palace back to Baghdad."

In a twinkling, the palace was back where it belonged and the Sultan was kissing his daughter and weeping tears of joy.

What a feast was held in the city that night! For thirty days all rejoiced, for the princess was well beloved throughout the land and Aladdin became as princely as though he had been born as a son to the Sultan himself.

And after a while, when the Sultan died, Aladdin was seated on the throne. He became a popular ruler who dealt justice to all. So he came to be loved by all the people of Baghdad . . . when Baghdad was still new.